The Penguin Who Wanted to Fly

To lovely Lola, Dolma, and Ross

ISBN 0-439-84244-1
Copyright © 2005 by Catherine Väse

All rights reserved. Published by Scholastic Inc., 557 Broadway, New York, NY 10012.
SCHOLASTIC and associated logos are trademarks and/or registered trademarks of Scholastic Inc.

12 11 10 9 8 7 6 5 4 3   6 7 8 9 10 11/0

Printed in the U.S.A.
First printing, January 2006

The Penguin Who Wanted to Fly

by
Catherine Vāse

SCHOLASTIC INC.

New York   Toronto   London   Auckland   Sydney
Mexico City   New Delhi   Hong Kong   Buenos Aires

Flip-Flop sat on his favorite thinking rock
and looked up at the sky.

"I wish I could fly," he said to himself.

Flip-Flop stood up. He looked down
at his wings and flapped them.
Nothing happened.
Flip-Flop couldn't fly.

That night Flip-Flop had a dream.
He dreamed he was flying.
It was so quiet and peaceful up there
in the starry sky.

The next morning, Flip-Flop had
an idea. He would make
himself some wings.

"Can I help?" asked Polar Bear.

Flip-Flop climbed on top of
Polar Bear and flapped his wings.
FLIP FLAP...

FLOP!

"OOPS!" said Flip-Flop.
But it didn't matter.
Flip-Flop had another idea.

"Just the thing," said Flip-Flop as he pulled out his special helicopter cap from his dress-up trunk.

He spun around and around and around and around and around and around and around and around, spinning faster and faster...

...until he spun out of control. "Ouch!" cried Flip-Flop as he flopped to the ground. "I feel very dizzy."

That night it snowed.

In the morning, Flip-Flop was very excited.

He had thought of another idea.

He would build an airplane
out of snow—a snow plane!

Flip-Flop was very pleased with himself as he climbed in.

5, 4, 3, 2, 1...

He waited for his snow plane to take off...
and waited...and waited.

"Oh dear!" Flip-Flop sighed
as the sun came out and melted
his snow plane.

But it didn't matter.
Flip-Flop had another idea—a better idea.

He got a balloon and tied
a piece of string to it.

The balloon floated upward,
and so did Flip-Flop!

"I'm flying,"
said Flip-Flop excitedly.
"I am really flying!"
And he was, until...

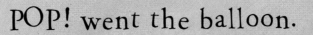
POP! went the balloon.

FLOP!
went Flip-Flop.
Poor Flip-Flop!

"I am never going to fly," he cried.

Polar Bear gave his friend a hug.
"Come with me," he said.

Polar Bear gave Flip-Flop a gentle push
down their favorite slide.

WHOOSH!

Flip-Flop whizzed down the ice.

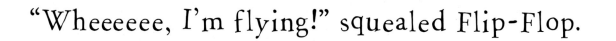

"Wheeeeee, I'm flying!" squealed Flip-Flop.

But then...

SPLASH!

"Help!" cried Flip-Flop
as he crashed into the sea.

It was very peaceful and quiet down there
under the sea. There were lots of fish
and other floaty things.

"Wow!" said Flip-Flop.
"This is just like flying!"

Flip-Flop couldn't really fly.
But that didn't matter, because Flip-Flop could swim.

In fact, he could swim quite beautifully.

Flip-Flop is a little penguin
with a big dream. He wants to fly!
But even his snow plane can't give him wings.
Then he discovers that wishes can come true—
sometimes in an unexpected way.

SCHOLASTIC

www.scholastic.com
This edition is only available for distribution through the school market.

ISBN 0-439-84244-1

EAN

9 780439 842440